FLUBBY

Flubby Is
Not
a Good Pet!

To the kind hearts at the Pat Brody Shelter for Cats—JEM

PENGUIN WORKSHOP
An Imprint of Penguin Random House LLC, New York

Copyright © 2019 by Jennifer Morris. All rights reserved. Previously published in hardcover in 2019 by Penguin Workshop. This paperback edition published in 2020 by Penguin Workshop, an imprint of Penguin Random House LLC, New York. PENGUIN and PENGUIN WORKSHOP are trademarks of Penguin Books Ltd, and the W colophon is a registered trademark of Penguin Random House LLC. Manufactured in China.

Visit us online at www.penguinrandomhouse.com.

Library of Congress Control Number: 2019005050

ISBN 9781524790783   10 9 8 7 6

Flubby Is
Not
a Good Pet!

by J. E. Morris

Penguin Workshop

This is Flubby.

He is my pet.

Kim has a pet.

Kim's pet can sing.

Flubby does not sing.

Sam has a pet.

Sam's pet can catch.

Catch, Flubby!
Catch the ball!

Flubby does not catch.

Jill has a pet.

Jill's pet can jump.

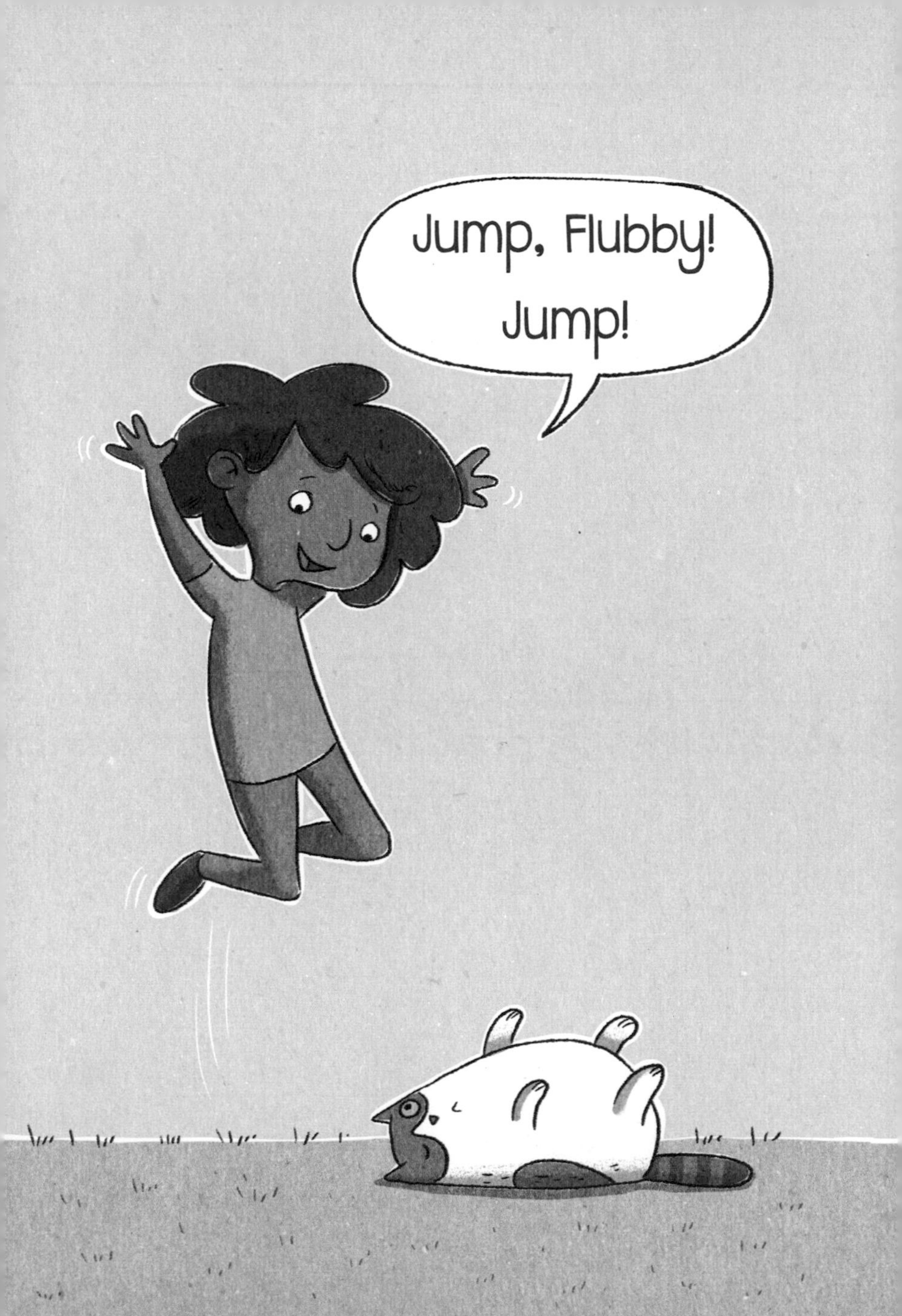
Jump, Flubby!
Jump!

Flubby does not jump.

Uh-oh.

Run, Flubby!
Run or you will get wet!

Flubby does not run.

No, Flubby! No!

Flubby does not sing.

Flubby does not catch.

Flubby does not jump.

Flubby does not run.

Flubby is NOT a good pet!

But he needs me.